panda series

**PANDA books are for first readers
beginning to make their own way
through books.**

HURRAY FOR THE PANDAS!

The PANDAS are now ten years old
and they have grown over the years.
There are now **34** books –
and lots of great **characters**:
you will meet many of them
in this book.
Have you read their stories?

CHECK OUT
THE FANTASTIC
PANDA SERIES

Panda Party

ANNA DONOVAN
•Pictures by Michael Connor•

THE O'BRIEN PRESS
DUBLIN

First published 2007 by The O'Brien Press Ltd,
12 Terenure Road East, Rathgar, Dublin 6, Ireland.
Tel: +353 1 4923333; Fax: +353 1 4922777
E-mail: books@obrien.ie
Website: www.obrien.ie

ISBN: 978-1-84717-028-6

British Library Cataloguing-in-Publication Data
Donovan, Anna
Panda party
1. Parties - Juvenile fiction 2. Children's stories
I. Title
823.9'14[J]

1 2 3 4 5 6 7 8 9 10
07 08 09 10 11 12

The O'Brien Press receives assistance from

the arts
council
schomhairle
ealaíon

Typesetting, layout, editing, design: The O'Brien Press Ltd
Printing: Cox & Wyman Ltd

Can YOU spot the panda
hidden in the story?

IT'S A PARTY!

'Hurray!' shouted Danny.
'Come on, Keeno. We're off
to the Panda Party.'

All the PANDA people
were going
and lots of PANDA animals too.

Katie had made
a special Panda Party cake.

Conor had practised
an amazing new piece
on the piano.

Conor's teacher was
in charge of the party.
She was dressed as

THE SHERIFF –

just in case there was trouble!

The party room was ready.
It was full of

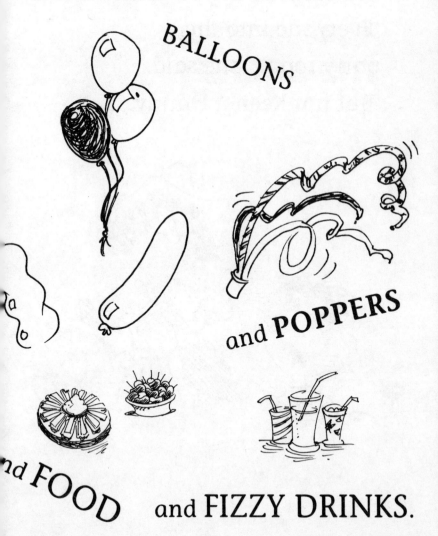

BALLOONS

and POPPERS

and FOOD

and FIZZY DRINKS.

9

THE SHERIFF stood up and shouted her orders: 'Everyone into the party room,' she said. 'But not Keeno, Danny.'

'No dogs allowed!'
said **THE SHERIFF**.
'Dogs are trouble!'

Danny stood in front of Keeno.
But **THE SHERIFF** saw Keeno.
'Out!' she shouted. 'Now!
We don't want **TROUBLE**!'

But she didn't see Lively.
Lively slipped in behind Jennie
and hid under a chair.
He stayed quiet – for once.

And she didn't see Polo.
He hid behind the
little black sheep.

Danny was NOT pleased.
It's not fair, he thought.
Keeno is more fun
than Lively or Polo.

He told Keeno to stay outside.

'Wait
here,'
he said.
'I'll call
you.'

The party started.
Conor played his
fantastic new piano tune.
It ripped up and down the keys
like a wave of sound.

Sinead and Tom danced
all around the room.
They crashed into a few people
on the way!

The ducks joined in the fun.
They played and sang:

'Ooh, la, booga BOMP!
BOMP! BOMP! BOMP!'

Then everyone started to
BOMP.

BOMP!

Muckeen bomped into Barry.
Barry went off to bed
with a sore head.

BOMP!

BOMP!

Lively bomped into Orlando.
Oh no!

Out came Orlando's
beautiful, polished claws.

BOMP!

Erin bomped into Freddy.
Sally bomped into Hannah.
Tom bomped into Tina.

IT WAS A MESS.

'**STOP**!'
shouted **THE SHERIFF**.
'Stop it, all of you.

This is a **mess**.
This is not a
proper party.'

She made them all sit down
quietly on the floor.

'Now, Erin will do
her party piece,'
said **THE SHERIFF**.

Erin held up her sharp scissors
and some coloured paper.
Snip! Snip! went the scissors.
Soon she had a long row
of dancing girls.

Everyone cheered.
'Hurray! Brilliant!'

'Now, who's next?'
asked **THE SHERIFF**.

'**ME**!' said a voice.
It was Danny.
He was wearing
a huge cloak.
'I'm a magician,' he said.

'Are you going to sing a song, Danny?' asked **THE SHERIFF**.
'Nope,' said Danny.
'I'm going to do a trick.'

He held up a tiny box.
'This tiny little box holds

a huge monster,' he said.

Oh no, thought **THE SHERIFF**.

I smell **TROUBLE**.

And she was right!

'Ab-ra-ca-dab-ra ...'
shouted Danny.
He waved the box
over his head.
He threw a fistful of stars
around the room.

He reached
under his cloak.

He took out a magic wand.

He pointed to the door.

He threw the little box
at the door.

'Abracadabra!' he shouted.

'**Keeno**!'

IN CAME KEENO.

'**WOOF!**' said Keeno.

'**Woof!**' said Lively.

'*Woof!*' said Polo.

'*Mieow!*' said Orlando.

'**Quack!**' said all the ducks.

'**Grunt!**' said Muckeen.

'Baa!' said the
little black sheep.

'Oh no,' said **THE SHERIFF**.

'**NO**. **NO**. **NO**.'

Katie was lighting
all the candles
on the special cake.
There was one candle
for every Panda book.
That was **34** candles.

Helpful Hannah helped her
to light them all.

'Hey!' called Sinead.
'Three cheers for Katie's
splendiferous cake.'

'**Hip hip hurray**!'
they all shouted.

The animals all dived
at the cake.

'**Stop**!' shouted Katie. '**Stop**!'

'**Stop**!' yelled Sinead.
'**STOP**!' roared Erin
and Tom and Freddy
and Hannah and Tina
and Conor and Sally
and Dara and Jennie.

'STOP!'

It was **THE SHERIFF**.

But none of them stopped.

The dogs fought with the cats.
The cats fought with the ducks.
The ducks fought with the goose.

IT WAS CHAOS!

'Those DOGS!
I knew they were trouble,'
said **THE SHERIFF**. 'I give up.'
She ran out the door.

'Hurray!' shouted Danny.
'Come on, Keeno.
Let's sort out this lot!'
But Danny and Keeno
only made things **worse**.

It was **PANDA-MONIUM!**

PANDA-

MONIUM

Then Sinead came in.

She was holding a long hose.

It was the **FIRE-HOSE**.

Sinead switched on
the fire-hose.
She sprayed water over
the whole lot of them.

Sinead drenched the dogs

and the cats
and the ducks
(who loved it)
and the goose
and little black sheep
and Katie and Conor

and all the others.

She drenched
Keeno and Danny.

Sinead drenched **everybody**.

They all ran from the room.

The party room was
a huge **MESS**.

And that was the end of the
PANDA PARTY.